LOOK AND FIND®
THE AMAZING
SPIDER-MAN®

LAYOUT ARTIST/ILLUSTRATION COORDINATOR: HOWARD BENDER
PENCILERS: HOWARD BENDER, RICH YANIZESKI, BRIAN CLOPPER, ALEX MORRISSEY, BRIAN BUNIAK
INKERS: DON HECK, MIKE ESPOSITO, MARIE SEVERIN
COLORISTS: NANSI HOOLAHAN, BRIAN BUNIAK, KEN FEDUNIEWICZ, TOM LUTH, TOM ZIUKO
COVER ARTIST: JEFF ALBRECHT STUDIOS

ILLUSTRATION SCRIPT DEVELOPMENT BY DWIGHT ZIMMERMAN

MARVEL, SPIDER-MAN, AND ALL RELATED CHARACTERS AND THE DISTINCT LIKENESSES
THEREOF ARE TRADEMARKS OF MARVEL CHARACTERS, INC., AND ARE USED WITH PERMISSION.
COPYRIGHT © 1992, 2006 MARVEL CHARACTERS, INC. ALL RIGHTS RESERVED.

WWW.MARVEL.COM

PUBLISHED BY LOUIS WEBER, C.E.O., PUBLICATIONS INTERNATIONAL, LTD.
7373 NORTH CICERO AVENUE, LINCOLNWOOD, ILLINOIS 60712
GROUND FLOOR, 59 GLOUCESTER PLACE, LONDON W1U 8JJ

CUSTOMER SERVICE: 1-800-595-8484 OR CUSTOMER_SERVICE@PILBOOKS.COM

WWW.PILBOOKS.COM

MANUFACTURED IN CHINA.

8 7 6 5 4 3 2 1

ISBN-13: 978-1-4127-6594-7
ISBN-10: 1-4127-6594-3

WLING WIMP!

WHILE SPIDEY'S DOING THAT, CAN YOU HELP HIM? MYSTERIO LEFT SOME CLUES TO SHOW WHERE THEY'RE GOING TO STRIKE FIRST.

SEE IF YOU CAN FIND THEM.

BEACH UMBRELLA

PICNIC BASKET

SURF BOARD

BEACH BALL

BUCKET AND SHOVEL

BEACH CHAIR

I, MYSTERIO, HAVE UNLEASHED THE ULTIMATE PLAN! NOT ONLY WILL MY CRIME SPREE TURN NEW YORK INTO A CITY OF CHAOS, IT WILL ALSO END IN THE DEFEAT OF MY GREATEST NEMESIS, SPIDER-MAN! ALREADY HE'S HOT ON MY TRAIL, BUT ONLY BECAUSE OF THE CLUES I LEFT FOR HIM. WITH A LITTLE HELP FROM ME, HE MIGHT OFFER ME AN AMUSING CHALLENGE.

MUSCLE
BEACH

SPIDER-MAN COULDN'T CATCH A FLY!

MUSSEL
BEACH

GO AHEAD, HELP HIM FIND THE CLUES
THAT REVEAL WHERE I WILL STRIKE NEXT.

HELP HIM MOVE ONE STEP CLOSER TO HIS
UNAVOIDABLE DEMISE!

COTTON
CANDY

TEDDY
BEAR

SHOOTING
GALLERY
DUCKS

ROLL OF
TICKETS

CAROUSEL
HORSE

FUN HOUSE
MIRROR

MYSTERIO IS STILL KEEPING ONE JUMP AHEAD OF ME, BUT I THINK HE'S RUNNING SCARED. I HAVE TO KEEP THE PRESSURE ON. SOONER OR LATER HE'LL MAKE A MISTAKE, AND THEN HE'LL BE OUT! I JUST HOPE IT'S SOONER, NOT LATER! IF I CAN FIND HIS CLUES, I'LL KNOW WHERE HE'S GOING TO STRIKE NEXT— AND BE THERE WAITING FOR HIM!

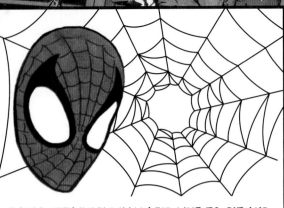

RADIO CITY MUSIC HALL! I'D LIKE TO SIT AND WATCH THE SHOW, BUT MYSTERIO IS MAKING THAT A LITTLE DIFFICULT FOR EVERYBODY. YOU'D THINK HE'D BE GETTING TIRED OF THIS BY NOW. I KNOW I AM. AS LONG AS HE'S OUT THERE CAUSING TROUBLE, I'LL BE OUT THERE PUTTING A STOP TO IT. I JUST WISH I COULD FIND A WAY TO PUT AN END TO THIS FOR GOOD.

MYSTERIO RULES

WHILE SPIDEY'S WORKING ON HIS PLAN, SEE IF YOU CAN FIND THESE THINGS THAT TELL WHERE MYSTERIO WILL GO FROM HERE.

THEATER MASKS

ACTOR

ACTRESS

COWBOY WITH LASSO

OPERA GLASSES

LION

TAXI

THERE CAN BE NO STOPPING US NOW. BETWEEN MYSTERIO'S CLONES AND THESE PEOPLE I HOLD UNDER MY VERY POWER, SPIDER-MAN STANDS NO CHANCE. AND IT'S SO FITTING THAT HIS END WILL BE BROUGHT ABOUT BY— HIMSELF!!

WIPE YOUR FEET, PLEASE

HOME SWEET CAVE

BUCKET O' CHICKEN

WELCOME TO THE SUBTERRANEAN LAIR

TO THE SURFACE

WC

TOUR

KEEP YOUR CAVERN CLEAN

Tunnel of Love

SOAP

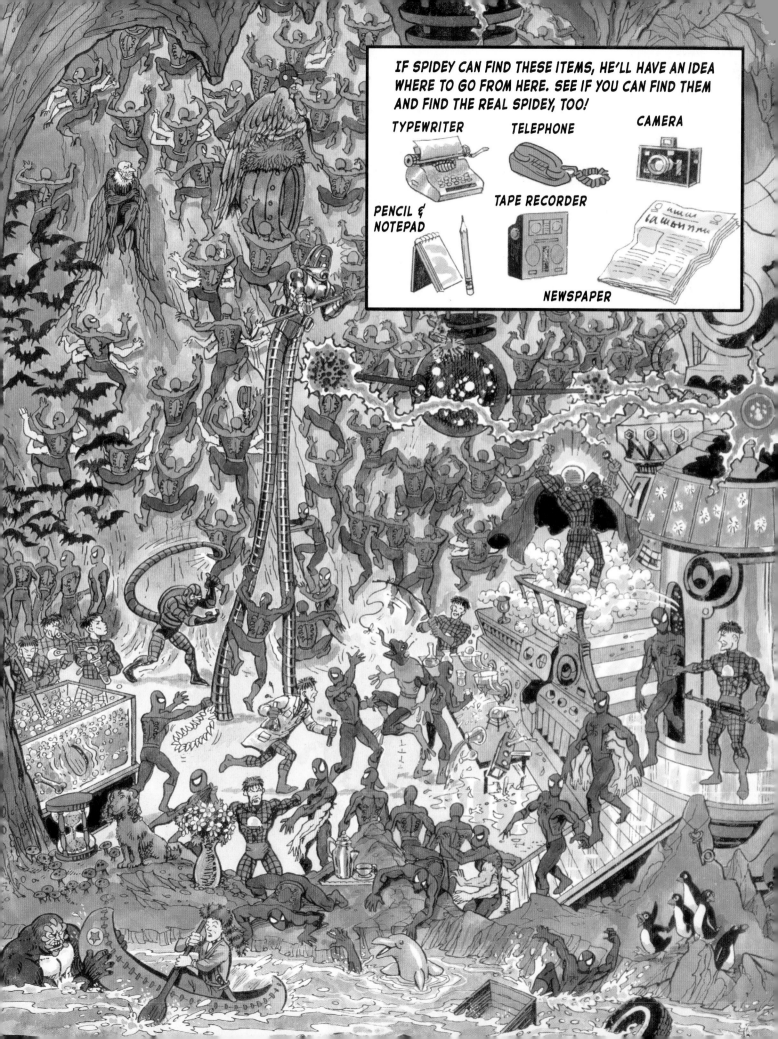

I HAD TO CALL IN A LOT OF DEBTS, BUT I'VE GOT SOME OLD FRIENDS HELPING ME OUT NOW. EVEN AFTER WE GET ALL THESE BAD GUYS UNDER CONTROL, THE WORK WON'T BE DONE. MYSTERIO HAS PLANTED EIGHT BOMBS IN THE CITY STREETS. WE HAVE TO FIND THEM, OR THERE'S NO TELLING HOW MANY PEOPLE WILL BE HURT!

SEARCH THE STREETS OUTSIDE THE BUGLE BUILDING FOR MYSTERIO'S DEVICES, AND THEN HOPE OUR HERO CAN DISARM THEM BEFORE THEY GO OFF.

IN ALL THE CONFUSION BACK AT THE DAILY BUGLE OFFICE, PETER PARKER LEFT SOME THINGS BEHIND. SEE IF YOU CAN FIND THEM FOR HIM.

- ❑ A SPIDER-MAN MASK
- ❑ A SPIDER-MAN SHIRT
- ❑ SPIDER-MAN TIGHTS
- ❑ SPIDER-MAN GLOVES
- ❑ SPIDER-MAN BOOTS
- ❑ SPIDER-MAN WEB SHOOTERS
- ❑ A CAMERA

THE MASTER OF ILLUSION AND SPECIAL EFFECTS HAS MISPLACED SOME OF HIS GEAR. GO BACK TO THE BEACH AND FIND THESE THINGS MYSTERIO USED TO PLAY HIS TRICKS.

- ❑ A MAGIC WAND
- ❑ A DECK OF CARDS
- ❑ A TOP HAT
- ❑ A WHITE RABBIT
- ❑ A MAKEUP KIT
- ❑ A PAIR OF HANDCUFFS
- ❑ A FAKE MUSTACHE

THE SCARLET WITCH HAS LEFT SOME OF HER ITEMS OF SORCERY BACK AT THE AMUSEMENT PARK. HELP HER TRACK THEM DOWN BEFORE THEY FALL INTO THE WRONG HANDS.

- ❑ A WITCH'S HAT
- ❑ A BROOM
- ❑ A BLACK CAT
- ❑ A BOOK OF MAGIC SPELLS
- ❑ A FROG PRINCE
- ❑ A CANDLE
- ❑ TOADSTOOLS

MATT MURDOCK LIKES TO SPEND QUITE A LOT OF TIME AT THE BALLPARK. GO BACK THERE AND TRY TO FIND THESE DARING AND DEVILISH ITEMS.

- ❑ DAREDEVIL LOGO
- ❑ DAREDEVIL'S BATON
- ❑ A GRAPPLING HOOK
- ❑ A PAIR OF SUNGLASSES
- ❑ A PITCHFORK
- ❑ A PAIR OF BOXING GLOVES

ALL THIS CRIMINAL ACTIVITY IS MAKING FROG-MAN HUNGRY. HAVE A LOOK AROUND RADIO CITY MUSIC HALL FOR THESE SUCCULENT TREATS HE'D LOVE TO GOBBLE UP.

- ❑ A SPIDER
- ❑ A FLY
- ❑ A BEETLE
- ❑ A CATERPILLAR
- ❑ A BUTTERFLY
- ❑ A GRASSHOPPER
- ❑ A WORM

WHEN THE NORSE GOD OF THUNDER VISITS TIMES SQUARE, YOU'LL KNOW THAT HE'S BEEN THERE. SEE IF YOU CAN FIND THESE THINGS THOR MIGHT HAVE LEFT BEHIND.

- ❑ A JACKHAMMER
- ❑ A CLAW HAMMER
- ❑ A SLEDGEHAMMER
- ❑ A VIKING HELMET
- ❑ A MODEL VIKING SHIP
- ❑ A SWORD AND A SHIELD

THE BAD GUYS HAVE LEFT STUFF SCATTERED ALL OVER THE BUILDING THAT LEADS TO THEIR SECRET BASE. SEARCH THE SINISTER WAREHOUSE FOR THEIR VILLAINOUS POSSESSIONS.

- ❑ ANI-MEN'S DOGGIE BAG
- ❑ BIRD-MAN'S TAIL FEATHER
- ❑ CAT-MAN'S CLAW BOOTS
- ❑ FROG-MAN'S FLIPPERS
- ❑ APE-MAN'S FUR BRUSH
- ❑ MYSTERIO'S GLASS HELMET
- ❑ CALYPSO'S NECKLACE
- ❑ SANDMAN'S BUCKET AND SHOVEL

CALYPSO HAS MAGIC TALISMANS STREWN ABOUT THE SECRET HIDEOUT. RETURN TO THE CAVERN AND FIND THESE MAGICAL OBJECTS.

- ❑ A SKULL
- ❑ A SHRUNKEN HEAD
- ❑ A VOODOO DOLL
- ❑ A RAVEN
- ❑ A BONE
- ❑ A DAGGER
- ❑ A GOLDEN CUP
- ❑ A TOOTH NECKLACE

MYSTERIO MAY BE A MENACE TO SOCIETY, BUT SOMETIMES SPIDEY'S GREATEST ENEMY IS J. JONAH JAMESON. LOOK AROUND THE STREET OUTSIDE THE DAILY BUGLE FOR THESE THINGS THAT BELONG TO JJJ.

- ❑ A BOX OF CIGARS
- ❑ A SPIDER-MAN DART BOARD
- ❑ A BRIEFCASE
- ❑ A BUNDLE OF NEWSPAPERS
- ❑ A POCKET WATCH
- ❑ A SUIT COAT

SO YOU FOUND THE BOMBS THAT MYSTERIO PLANTED OUTSIDE THE DAILY BUGLE.
GOOD WORK, BUT IF THEY AREN'T ALSO DISARMED, THE CITY WILL STILL BE DEVASTATED. LUCKILY, MYSTERIO HAS LEFT A WAY TO AVERT THE CATASTROPHE. EACH OF THE OTHER EIGHT PLACES HE VISITED HAS A HIDDEN KEY THAT WILL DEFUSE ONE OF THE BOMBS. GO BACK TO THE LOCATIONS, FIND THE KEYS, AND MATCH THEM WITH THE CORRECT BOMBS.